D0953502

MAXIMILIAN P. MOUSE, TIME TRAVELER

PATRIOTIC MOUSE

BOSTON TEA PARTY PARTICIPANT

BOOK 1

Philip M. Horender • Guy Wolek

visit us at www.abdopublishing.com

To my wife Erin, whose love and support helped give Maximilian to us all —PMH

Published by Magic Wagon, a division of the ABDO Group, PO Box 398166, Minneapolis, Minnesota 55439. Copyright © 2014 by Abdo Consulting Group, Inc. International copyrights reserved in all countries. All rights reserved. No part of this book may be reproduced in any form without written permission from the publisher.

Calico Chapter Books™ is a trademark and logo of Magic Wagon.

Printed in the United States of America, North Mankato, Minnesota.
052013
092013
 This book contains at least 10% recycled materials.

Text by Philip M. Horender
Illustrations by Guy Wolek
Edited by Stephanie Hedlund and Rochelle Baltzer
Cover and interior design by Neil Klinepier

Library of Congress Cataloging-in-Publication Data
Horender, Philip M.
  Patriotic mouse : Boston Tea Party participant / by Philip M. Horender ; illustrated by Guy Wolek.
     p. cm. -- (Maximilian P. Mouse, time traveler ; bk. 1)
  Summary: In an attempt to save his family's oak tree home, Maximilian uses Nathaniel Chipmunk's time machine to try and prevent Farmer Tanner from selling the property to a developer, but finds himself more than two centuries in the past, in the middle of the Boston Tea Party, instead.
  ISBN 978-1-61641-957-8
1. Mice--Juvenile fiction. 2. Boston Tea Party, Boston, Mass., 1773--Juvenile fiction. 3. Time travel--Juvenile fiction. 4. United States--History--Colonial period, ca. 1600-1775--Juvenile fiction. 5. Boston (Mass.)--History--Colonial period, ca. 1600-1775--Juvenile fiction. [1. Mice--Fiction. 2. Animals--Fiction. 3. Boston Tea Party, Boston, Mass., 1773--Fiction. 4. Time travel--Fiction. 5. Adventure and adventurers--Fiction. 6. United States--History--Colonial period, ca. 1600-1775--Fiction. 7. Boston (Mass.)--History--Colonial period, ca. 1600-1775--Fiction.] I. Wolek, Guy, ill. II. Title.
  PZ7.H78087Pat 2013
  813.6--dc23   2012050545

TABLE OF
CONTENTS

Chapter 1:
MY DEAREST SON

A cool, crisp breeze blew through the lazy willow trees. This breeze marked the change in seasons. It swept away the longer, carefree summer days. Now the autumn months for winter preparation were blowing into Tanner's Glen.

A small field mouse sat perched on an old ash log in the middle of the glen. He gazed about in wonder and thought of this change of seasons.

He was a handsome field mouse, small yet **distinguished**. His silky gray coat was **offset** by his long whiskers. This field mouse was lost in his thoughts. He watched leaves float underneath darkening clouds. He had completely lost track of the time.

A strong gust chilled the small mouse and he pulled his **waistcoat** tight. Just then, the

familiar chime of his pocket watch sang out. He carefully removed the watch from his breast pocket and opened it.

It was six o'clock. The mouse thought about his family and wondered what they were doing at that moment. He knew his mother would be preparing supper. She would worry if he were any later.

Maximilian ran his paw over the **engraving** on the polished, silver pocket watch case. It said: *To My Dearest Son, Maximilian P. Mouse.*

This watch was his most **cherished** possession. His father had given it to him on his first birthday. That was just before he disappeared. Maximilian wondered where his father could be. He hoped he was safe.

Maximilian finally noticed how quickly the weather was changing. He jumped to the ground and disappeared into the woods. A storm was building and Maximilian needed to get home soon.

He scurried down a beaten path. He and his mother had walked it when they had collected blackberries months ago. Even though the long blades of the sweetgrass blocked his view, Maximilian knew the way by heart.

Up ahead he could make out the warm glow of a single candle. Its light was **emanating** from the oak tree the Mouse family called home.

The oak tree was one of the largest and most impressive in the woods. It had survived countless storms mostly unharmed. It was the only home Maximilian had ever known.

Maximilian sped up. He wanted to get inside before the storm hit. He knew his mother would worry terribly if he or his younger sister, Sally, were out when the rains came.

Soon, Maximilian had reached the front door. As he pushed the door open, huge drops of rain began to fall. He was just in time. But he wasn't prepared for what he found inside.

Chapter 2:
NEWS OF THE GLEN

Maximilian could hear the fire licking the kettle in the fireplace. The oak tree was warm and cozy. Maximilian hung his coat on a nail next to the door.

The house was quiet. His younger sister was putting together a puzzle next to the **hearth**. His mother was cutting carrots in the kitchen. Although the house was dimly lit, Maximilian could see that his mother's eyes were red and swollen. It looked as if she had been crying.

"Is everything alright, Mother?" Maximilian asked, sitting down at the table.

"Oh, Maximilian, I don't know what we will do," she said. Tears were beginning to build in her eyes.

Maximilian's mother had spent many evenings crying since his father had gone missing. He could hear her sobbing at night as he was trying to fall asleep.

It had been almost a full year now since Father had not returned from gathering straw and bedding. Mother had held on to hope that he would return to them.

Maximilian had searched for his father every day for weeks. But he found nothing. He often found himself sitting on the same ash tree thinking life would never be the same again. He had accepted his new role as mouse of the house. He took that role very seriously. So, it pained him greatly to see his mother this upset.

"I don't understand," he said. "What's wrong?"

Mother sat next to him at the table. She leaned over and placed her paw over his.

"This afternoon Bartholomew Squirrel stopped in. He told us Farmer Tanner is losing the farm," she said in a low, sad voice.

"How can that be?" Maximilian asked in amazement. "This farm and its land have been in his family for as long as the oak tree has been in ours. Why would he want to sell it?"

Maximilian thought for a moment. He finally said, "Maybe another farmer will buy it. Maybe he will use it just as Farmer Tanner has. Maybe this won't really affect us at all." Maximilian hoped to calm his mother's nerves. She shook her head sadly.

"The farm isn't being sold, Maximilian. The bank is foreclosing on it," she explained. "That means that Farmer Tanner is behind on his payments and the bank is taking his farm from him."

Mother sighed. She continued her story by saying, "Bartholomew overheard Farmer Tanner speaking with the realtor. The land is being purchased by a development group that plans on leveling the entire glen." Mother broke down and put her face in her paws.

Maximilian was growing more concerned. What would his family do? They had no other place to go.

His mother dabbed her eyes with her towel. She rose from her chair and continued making dinner. A worried Maximilian went to his room, lay down, and listened to the storm outside.

The rain continued to pelt the windows. But, Maximilian wasn't paying attention to the rain. He was focused on lacing up his shoes. He grabbed the backpack that he had filled with sunflower seeds, a **canteen**, and a compass.

Maximilian's parents had always warned him of the dangers in the woods at night. It was perfectly clear that he was never to leave the oak tree once darkness had fallen on Tanner's Glen.

But tonight, Maximilian had to face the danger in order to save his home. He lit a small lantern. He threw the backpack over his shoulder and took a final glance back at the bedroom. He sent a silent good-bye to the room where his mother and sister lay asleep. Then, he opened the door and disappeared into the night.

Chapter 3:
DANGER IN THE MOONLIGHT

By now, it had been raining for several hours. Maximilian had all he could do to avoid the large puddles along the path. One slip and he could find himself in a serious **predicament**.

Maximilian didn't have a plan really. But, he knew that doing nothing would result in losing his home. As mouse of the house, he had to do something.

Maximilian knew the importance of using the underbrush as protection. Owls and other birds of prey were almost certainly out hunting for their next meal. As he walked, the moon's light began to slowly break through the clouds and the rain began to lessen.

The determined mouse stopped briefly under a bush. He straightened his pack and wiped his brow. The sweat stung his eyes. He was suddenly reminded of how tired he was.

Maximilian was also worried. He knew his mother would be frightened when she awoke to discover he was gone. He had left a note on the kitchen table, but he knew it would provide little comfort. Whatever he was going to do, it had to be done quickly.

As the rain stopped, an **eerie** silence fell over the woods. Out of the corner of his eye, Maximilian caught a glimpse of movement. Then, he saw the glow of two yellow eyes.

Maximilian's heart began pounding. He had never actually seen an owl before. But he'd heard enough stories. He knew that it was an owl that sat in the far pine tree. And that owl had him in its sights.

Maximilian felt faint. He strained to keep himself focused on his next move. He fought the urge to run as fast as he could back the way he came. After all, he knew that his speed would be no match for the swift owl.

Maximilian wanted to be back home. He wanted his mother. He had done a very selfish thing by leaving her alone. Now Maximilian feared she and his sister would be on their own once again.

Suddenly, a soft voice spoke behind Maximilian. He was unsure where the voice was coming from, but it calmed his nerves immediately.

"You've gotten yourself in a delicate situation, my friend," the voice said softly. "Take a deep breath. Five yards straight ahead is a pine tree. At its base is the entrance to a tunnel. When I tell you to, run as fast as the wind to that tunnel, you understand?"

Maximilian nodded and fought the urge to cry. He could hear his heart beating in his ears.

"Now!" the voice instructed.

Maximilian sprang from the bush and sprinted into the clearing. As he ran,

Maximilian could see the owl swoop from the tree. Its razor-sharp **talons** glistened in the moonlight.

Maximilian pumped his arms and prayed that the tunnel opening would be where he was told. The owl was closing in fast. Maximilian made a desperate leap toward the tree's base and braced himself for whatever happened next.

Chapter 4:
NATHANIEL CHIPMUNK III

Maximilian narrowly escaped the owl's grasp as he tumbled head over heels into a long, narrow tunnel.

Once inside, he collected himself. He stepped away from the tunnel's entrance and stared down the dimly lit walkway. Candleholders decorated the walls, hanging several feet apart from one another. The melted wax from the candles traced its way down to the floor.

Maximilian adjusted his overcoat and walked deeper into the tunnel. With each step he took, the entrance became smaller and smaller behind him.

"Where am I?" Maximilian said aloud, hoping he didn't receive a response.

Finally, he came to a small wooden door. A finely polished bronze knocker was securely positioned in its center. A sign hung around the knocker. Maximilian squinted in the poor lighting to make out the words. It said:

Acquaintances knock once,
Twice for strangers,
Then wipe your feet and
come in out of danger.

Maximilian followed the directions and knocked twice. The door slowly swung open.

Peering inside, Maximilian said, "Hello? Is anyone there?"

He stepped inside and the door closed. The room was decorated with countless maps, puzzles, books, and globes. Maximilian stood in the center of the room and turned in circles, trying to take in all the wonder it had to offer.

Maximilian was so preoccupied, he didn't notice a figure place itself next to an end table. The figure pulled the chain to a lamp covered by a stained glass shade. It threw a wave of colors onto the room's ceiling.

"Please, have a seat," the familiar voice said, motioning with his paw to a couch.

Maximilian jumped, startled that he wasn't alone. For the first time, he saw the animal who had saved him in the glen.

A chipmunk with wire-rimmed glasses sat comfortably in the leather chair across from him. He was an older chipmunk, with some of the fur around his whiskers turning gray. He impressed Maximilian as being very scholarly, kind of like Mr. Jacob W. Mouse, his schoolteacher.

"My apologies for not introducing myself earlier," the chipmunk said with a chuckle. "My name is Nathaniel Chipmunk III. It is my pleasure to be making your **acquaintance**."

"My name is Maximilian P. Mouse. I owe you my life," Maximilian replied.

Nathaniel repositioned himself. He used the sleeve of his sweater to polish the lens of his glasses.

"My fine young man, you must certainly be aware of the dangers present at this hour. I cannot imagine why a sharp-witted mouse such as yourself was willing to ignore such risks."

Maximilian placed his backpack on the couch next to him. Then, he told Nathaniel everything.

He began with how the old oak tree had been in his family for generations. Then he explained that his father had gone missing the year before. He spoke about Farmer Tanner and how the bank was going to take his property if nothing was done. And finally, Maximilian talked about how it was his responsibility, as his father's only son, to fix the problem.

Nathaniel listened closely. Maximilian felt comfortable talking with Nathaniel. It felt good to tell his story to someone.

When his entire story ended, Maximilian sat quietly. He was curious as to how his new friend would respond. Nathaniel's expression gave him no clues.

"That's quite the tale," Nathaniel said. He removed his glasses and rubbed his eyes.

"I think I can help you," he finally said. "But you're going to have to trust me."

"You saved my life once already," Maximilian responded. "You've earned my trust."

"Good," Nathaniel said, nodding. "Good. The first order of business is for you to get some much-needed rest. It's far too dangerous for you to continue your journey tonight. You'll need all the energy you have come dawn."

Nathaniel got to his feet and took Maximilian's bag. "Come, I've prepared the guest room for you."

He led Maximilian through a maze of hallways. Finally, they made their way up a short flight of stairs to a simple room with a bed, nightstand, and rocking chair.

"Here you are, lad," Nathaniel said. He placed Maximilian's belongings on the floor. "I'm sure you'll find the linens crisp and the pillow soft."

"Thank you for everything," Maximilian said.

"No, Maximilian," Nathaniel said gently, "thank you."

When the chipmunk had left, Maximilian sat on the bed. Nathaniel was right. The down-filled mattress and finely stitched pillows were very comfortable. Maximilian carefully placed his pocket watch on the nightstand and blew out the lantern.

Chapter 5:
THE ANSWER

Maximilian was awakened by the smell of fresh-baked corn bread and the faint whistle of a teakettle. The smell of the corn bread practically carried him to the kitchen. There, he found Nathaniel pouring himself a cup of tea.

"I trust you slept alright," Nathaniel said.

Maximilian nodded. "Yes, everything was perfect. Thank you, Nathaniel. I'm just very worried about my mother, that's all."

"Ah, yes, your troubles. They occupied my mind for most of the night as well," Nathaniel said. He cut a piece of bread and placed it on a plate in front of Maximilian.

"What would you say if I told you that you could save Tanner's Glen without leaving your mother and sister for one second?" he asked. "What would you say to that, my fine fellow?"

"I don't understand—" Maximilian began. But Nathaniel interrupted him.

"Of course you don't," Nathaniel said. "What I've just suggested seems impossible! Finish your breakfast and I'll explain."

Maximilian finished two pieces of corn bread. Just after he helped himself to a second cup of tea, Nathaniel handed him a jacket. Then, the chipmunk led Maximilian to a set of stairs outside of his study.

The stairway had an **intricately** carved **banister**. Maximilian watched as Nathaniel pulled a hidden lever. A series of gears could be heard as the stairway moved along the hardwood floor. Suddenly, they revealed a hidden passage! Maximilian couldn't believe his eyes.

"Please be careful on these stairs. They can be frightfully slippery from the dampness," Nathaniel warned. "Watch your step."

Nathaniel led Maximilian down the winding basement steps, deeper and deeper into the earth. Maximilian slid his paw across the stone wall, using it for support as he went.

The stairs emptied into a large workroom. It was nothing like the study. This room was decorated with tools for carpentry, drafting, and woodwork. Numerous blueprints, compasses, rulers, and textbooks lay strewn on the floor.

"This is it!" Nathaniel exclaimed.

Maximilian paused then said, "What *is* it?"

Nathaniel let out a hearty laugh.

"Are all of these tools yours?" Maximilian asked.

"Yes, well, technically speaking," Nathaniel said. "I **inherited** them from my grandfather. They originally belonged to him. It took him a painfully long time to collect them all."

Maximilian began to wander through the room.

"This is your answer, Maximilian," Nathaniel continued. "The answer to all of your problems." He placed his paws in his pockets and sat on a stool in the corner.

"I don't see how this can possibly help me save Tanner's Glen," Maximilian said disappointedly.

"Let me explain," Nathaniel said. "My grandfather was a dreamer, if you will. Much like you and me really." At this point, Nathaniel was back on his feet.

"He spent his life reading books and applying the knowledge of others. He had one goal. That goal occupied his days and nights." Nathaniel paused until Maximilian was staring at him.

"Time travel, my small friend," he said. "Time travel."

Chapter 6:
THE TIME MACHINE

Maximilian looked at Nathaniel in amazement.

"Did your grandfather actually develop a way to travel through time?" Maximilian asked in a whisper. His heart was pounding.

Nathaniel motioned for Maximilian to come closer. He leaned toward him, whispering as if he didn't want anyone overhearing.

"He did," Nathaniel said. "My grandfather kept **meticulous** notes for his dream time machine. He didn't complete the machine he planned. But I took on his task as my own. The sketches and notes Grandfather made put him on the brink of time travel," Nathaniel said.

Maximilian's eyes were **transfixed** on a covered object in the far corner of the room.

"So he never actually traveled in time?" Maximilian asked.

Nathaniel retrieved a leather-bound diary from a shelf over his worktable. He carefully opened the book.

He cleared his throat and read aloud, "Upon completion of the outer shell, I have, by chance, discovered the necessary ingredient for fueling the capsule—onion juice. It is safe to say that this will help the chipmunk community **transcend** time and space . . ."

Nathaniel had Maximilian's undivided attention now. He moved to the mystery object in the corner and pulled on the sheet. It fell to the floor, revealing a large egg-shaped capsule.

"The outer shell is an acorn," Nathaniel explained. "Surprisingly, it is able to withstand the intense cold during time travel." He ran his hand over the dark frame as he talked.

Maximilian swallowed hard and asked, "There is intense cold?"

Nathaniel nodded and kept talking. "I polished the acorn with onion juice," he laughed. "It seems the onion juice does something to help offset the **friction.** This keeps the capsule on course. Without it, the capsule would fly off track. Onion juice is also the time machine's fuel."

Nathaniel stood admiring the time machine.

"You don't expect me to operate this machine, do you, Nathaniel?" Maximilian asked.

Nathaniel finally glanced up at Maximilian. "Why, of course," he said calmly.

Maximilian stared at him. He stammered, "But, I don't have a clue how it works. I'm just a field mouse."

"My fellow," Nathaniel said, "you merely set the proper coordinates and enjoy the ride!"

"Can't you go with me?" Maximilian asked.

"Sorry, chap, it's only designed for one time traveler," Nathaniel said. "You'll be fine. After all, there isn't another option. Do you know of any **alternatives**?"

Maximilian thought for a moment. He looked at the time machine just as his pocket watch chimed seven.

"How does it work?" he finally asked.

Chapter 7:
DESTINATION: TANNER'S GLEN

Maximilian sat quietly on a wooden stool, trying to concentrate.

"These gauges don't need to worry you. All you have to worry about is this display." Nathaniel pointed to a panel on his left that had the words *Year, Month, Day,* and *Destination* carefully stenciled above it.

"All of the numbers are digital to help ensure there is no confusion," Nathaniel said. "We'll set this first time together and send you back two weeks or so. That should give you time to get to Farmer Tanner's and be there when he meets with the developing group."

Maximilian nodded.

"Whatever happens, you have to keep that deal from being made. How you do that, is in your paws," Nathaniel said.

Maximilian nodded again. He could feel butterflies fluttering in his stomach.

"Now, there are some very important details I need to tell you," Nathaniel continued. "Once you have been transported in the time machine, you will not be able to use it again for twenty-four hours. The core needs time to reenergize and the protective shield needs time to cool."

Maximilian nodded again. "Twenty-four hours," he repeated. "Got it."

"Also, it's extremely important that at no point you come into contact with the you of the past," he warned sternly. "It's **imperative!** The results of that could be **catastrophic!**"

Maximilian was forced to repeat that last piece of information back to Nathaniel. Nathaniel wanted to make sure Maximilian had heard and understood him. When he was finally convinced, it was time for Maximilian to get into the time machine.

Maximilian slowly approached a wooden stepladder decorated with various paint drippings. With a deep breath, he carefully climbed through the portal. He sat in the leather-upholstered driver's seat and buckled the harness.

Nathaniel leaned into the window and extended his paw toward Maximilian.

Maximilian, although quite restrained with the seat belts and harnesses, stiffly took Nathaniel's paw and grasped it hard.

"Good luck, my brave little mouse," Nathaniel said. "I'll see you soon."

Maximilian's nerves were relieved somewhat by the chipmunk's firm, confident handshake.

It has to be done, Maximilian kept repeating over and over in his head. He watched Nathaniel secure the hatch from the outside. Then, he looked at the coordinates one last time:

2013, October, 15, Tanner's Glen.

He swallowed hard and squeezed his eyes shut.

The time capsule began to spin. Then, it sped up. Maximilian strained to keep his sight on the control panel in front of him. Beads of sweat were forming on his forehead as the temperature began to rise inside the time machine.

Maximilian fought the urge to get sick to his stomach. The time machine went faster and faster.

Just when Maximilian felt as though he couldn't take any more . . . it slowly came to a stop.

Chapter 8:
LOST

Maximilian opened his eyes. They were sore from how hard he had pressed them together.

From his seat, he could see smoke clearing in front of the portal. Had it worked? Where was he?

Maximilian cautiously unbuckled his belt and harness and sat forward. He grabbed the latch to the portal and quickly let go. It was cold—freezing really. Maximilian drew his paw back in pain.

He was more nervous than he had ever been before. A part of him wanted to sit back down and stay in the time machine. However, the other part of him, the part that had willed him on this journey in the first place, wouldn't allow it.

Maximilian took a handkerchief from his breast pocket and used it to open the latch. There was a pop as the airtight suction was broken. Maximilian stuck his nose through the door and slowly peered out.

It was dark outside and the air smelled stale. Maximilian carefully climbed out and jumped onto a dirt floor.

His pulse was beginning to return to normal. Maximilian looked for clues that might give him an idea of where the time machine had taken him. He noticed large bricks and support beams around him. He glanced up and found large wooden planks above him.

At first, Maximilian thought he had been transported directly under Farmer Tanner's farmhouse. Not bad luck considering all the other places he could have ended up. It was relatively safe and he could stay there until it was time to launch his plan with Farmer Tanner.

Launch the plan . . . It dawned on him that he really hadn't thought of that until now. How on earth could he keep Farmer Tanner from losing the farm?

Maximilian decided to take a closer look around. He would think about that question some more later. He walked to the foundation and looked upward.

Maximilian could hear voices. They were faint, but he was fairly sure he could hear a conversation directly above him.

He scurried to an old pile of bricks and climbed up them. He carefully dodged cobwebs as he went. Climbing higher, it became clear that the voices were of two men. They were engaged in a rather heated **debate**.

Was Farmer Tanner already meeting with the development group? Was he too late?

Maximilian reached the top and could see the men through a gap in the plank floor. He strained his ears to make out what they were saying.

"I'm just a little worried that's all, Samuel," a stocky gentleman said. He was pacing back and forth nervously.

Samuel had to be the older man in the chair next to Maximilian. He was sitting with one leg propped up on his other knee.

"Relax, Ebenezer," Samuel said. Maximilian liked the confidence in his voice.

"Relax? Relax? How can I relax while those three ships lay anchored in our own harbor, laden with tea? How can I relax when decent men like John Hancock and myself cannot get a single barrel through the British **tariff**?"

Ebenezer continued to pace. He was young, but he looked tired and pale. "How can I possibly relax when at any time it could be my neck that's fitted for a noose to be hung from a tree in the city square?" he continued.

Maximilian was growing more and more confused.

"Ebenezer, you'll wear a trench in these floorboards if you don't cease with all of this pacing," Samuel joked. The expression on Ebenezer's face showed that he was in no mood for joking.

"Honestly, my good friend," Samuel began, noticing his colleague's grim appearance, "you must have faith in the plan set forth in today's meeting. Things have a way of working out.

"We both know that as the winter months approach, King George and his lobster-back **regiments** have no desire to have this bickering drawn out any more," Samuel finished.

Ebenezer paused, and the first sign of relief crept across his face. "You're right, my good friend," he said, managing a slight smile. "You always are."

As Maximilian tried to process all that he was seeing, he noticed that another party was present. At the foot of Samuel's desk sat a brown mouse, frantically taking notes.

The mouse's elegant feather quill pen was sweeping madly across his scroll. He paused only twice to put his pen to his lips and scratch his brow. A number of additional scrolls lay neatly next to him. Maximilian thought of all the work and time that must have gone into each one.

As Ebenezer and Samuel finished their conversation, the brown mouse rubbed his eyes from exhaustion. His glasses were removed from his forehead and positioned back on his nose.

The mouse placed his pen in its inkwell. He gathered all of the scrolls in his arms and walked slowly out of the room. Maximilian watched as the mouse balanced the pen and ink **precariously** in his paw.

When the mouse was out of sight, Maximilian climbed back to the ground. One thing had become quite clear to him—he was not in Tanner's Glen. But where exactly was he?

Chapter 9:
A NEW FRIEND

Maximilian went back to the time machine. He sat on the dirt and leaned against it. It was still cold to the touch, but Maximilian didn't care. He had more important matters on his mind.

Where was he? And how was he going to save Tanner's Glen now?

Suddenly, Maximilian heard a rustling behind him. The noise was soon followed by a deep sigh of frustration.

"Oh, bother," a voice said pathetically.

"Hello?" Maximilian called out.

After a moment, Maximilian's call was answered by, "If you wouldn't mind lending a paw . . ."

Maximilian stood quickly. He walked toward the **silhouette** of the mouse he had seen upstairs.

When Maximilian took three scrolls in his arms, he could finally see the brown mouse.

"A thousand thank yous," the brown mouse said. "My name's Bigby, Oliver W. Bigby." He peered at Maximilian through his glasses. "And you are?" Oliver asked.

"I am Maximilian P. Mouse," Maximilian replied. He walked next to Oliver and added, "And I happen to be very lost."

"Lost are ya?" Oliver said. He motioned for Maximilian to follow him to a table in the corner. The table had a **blotter** on it and it looked like it was used often.

Oliver spoke with an accent that Maximilian hadn't heard before. But it seemed to fit his jolly appearance just right.

"Where might you be from?" Oliver continued. "That might be a good place to start in determining just how lost you really are."

"I'm from Tanner's Glen," Maximilian answered. He placed the scrolls carefully on the table, catching one as it began rolling back toward the ground.

"Tanner's Glen . . . Tanner's . . . Tanner's," Oliver repeated, like an echo. "I can't say that I'm familiar with any Tanner's Glen," Oliver finally said. "Might that be anywhere near our beloved Commonwealth of Virginia?"

Maximilian shrugged. He didn't know where the Commonwealth of Virginia was! The situation was looking worse and worse. Maximilian was becoming very worried.

"Because if it is, you are indeed a long way from home. Anyhow, I imagine you are probably **famished**," he chuckled. "Follow me and I'll fix us some supper."

Maximilian sat on an empty spool of thread. He was on the same dirt floor that he and the time machine had touched down on hours earlier.

Oliver was nearby tending to a small fire. He often stirred a kettle that was carefully suspended over the flames.

"This is a family recipe, handed down from generation to generation," Oliver said. "It is guaranteed to make your whiskers curl and your stomach smile." He laughed again and put Maximilian at ease.

"So, what brings you to Boston, Maximilian?" Oliver inquired.

"Boston?" Maximilian responded. "I didn't realize that's where I was."

Oliver took a break from stirring. "Indeed! You are in the largest city on this side of the Mississippi River, I reckon."

Oliver handed Maximilian a plate and a spoon. Then, he scooped some of the meal he had prepared onto the plate. It smelled good. Maximilian hadn't eaten anything since Nathaniel's breakfast earlier that morning and he was famished.

How long ago had that really been? Maximilian wondered.

"I'm confused," Maximilian said. "I think there has been a terrible mistake. I'm supposed to be in Tanner's Glen."

"My friend, I've lived here my entire life," Oliver said, "and I have never heard of such a place."

When Oliver glanced up, he noticed that the look on Maximilian's face was becoming more and more worried. He quickly asked, "What's so important that you need to find Tanner's Glen?"

Maximilian began to tell his story. He told it exactly as he had told it to Nathaniel the night before. Each time he recounted it, he felt more and more desperate.

Maximilian left out any mention of a time-traveling machine for the time being. He was having a hard time believing that part of his story. He wasn't sure how he would explain it to someone else.

Oliver listened carefully. When Maximilian was finished, he placed a small blade of straw in his mouth and sat back on his spool.

"Let me get this straight," Oliver said. "I want to make absolutely sure that I know what you're saying to me. This farmer of yours just up and sold your home without so much as a warning or a meeting? He didn't ask what you fine folks might think of the whole situation?"

"That's right, Oliver," said Maximilian. "Not just my home, but the homes of dozens other animals just like me."

Oliver shook his head in disgust. "That's just not right," he said sternly. "Awfully ironic though, I have to say."

"How's that?" asked Maximilian.

"Well, we here in Boston—all of the colonies for that matter—are facing the identical situation you folks are," he said. His voice started to rise in volume. "Except our Farmer Tanner is a fine old fat cat named King George, who's all the way over in England! How do you like that? He doesn't even live near us! He's an entire ocean away."

By this time, Oliver was becoming more and more animated. He had jumped to his feet and was waving his arms around. It was becoming clear to Maximilian that Oliver was also dissatisfied with his problem. The two mice certainly shared the same enthusiasm,

not to mention frustration, over their current situations.

"This King George seems to think he has the power to **levy** all sorts of taxes on us living here in the colonies," Oliver explained. "Taxes on stamps, taxes on playing cards, taxes on tea! What is this world coming to?"

Oliver rolled his eyes in amazement. "A mouse can't sit down after a hard day's work and enjoy a cup of tea without having to pay paw over fist for it!"

"And you have no say in any of this?" Maximilian asked.

"None!" Oliver declared. "Whatever King George and **Parliament** says goes."

Maximilian nodded in agreement.

"My friend, it has been like this for years, I am sorry to report," Oliver said. "First the Brits passed the **Sugar Act.** We complained. Then they levied the **Stamp Act.** We threw up our paws.

"Instead of doing what was right, they passed the **Townshend Acts**. And believe you me, while it is difficult to pronounce, it is easy to feel the effects of it in one's purse! Finally, they forced the **Tea Acts** on us. This time, I'm sure the boys will do more than just fling words Britain's way."

Oliver adjusted some of the fire's coals. Maximilian thought he must have been trying to calm himself down.

"Are the boys you're referring to the ones I saw you listening in on earlier?" Maximilian pried.

"One and the same," Oliver replied. "They are members of the Sons of Liberty. They are men who have taken up the torch to deal with such **injustices**, you might say. The gentlemen you saw were Boston's own Samuel Adams and Mr. Ebenezer McIntosh."

Oliver turned toward Maximilian and continued, "I've taken it upon myself for some time now to act as **scribe** for such meetings. Then, I am able to properly inform the members of my district as to what the Sons of Liberty are discussing," he said proudly. "I like to keep my members up to date on every detail that is discussed."

Oliver looked at Maximilian. He paused as if he were posing for his portrait to be painted. He waited for Maximilian to ask the question he was wanting to answer.

"What are they planning, Oliver?" Maximilian asked. "They seemed pretty excited when I heard them before."

"Well, what exactly, I myself am not privy to. But I can tell you it's going to be grand for sure," Oliver whispered. "It has to be for the British to realize that we colonists mean business!"

Chapter 10:
1773!

Maximilian noticed the sun was beginning to rise on a new day. It dawned on him that he had lost all concept of time.

"Look at that!" exclaimed Oliver. "We've been talking all evening, like two old mice."

Maximilian's mind crept back to something Nathaniel had told him. *Once you have been transported in the time machine, you will not be able to use it again for twenty-four hours.*

"Maximilian?" Oliver repeated.

Maximilian shook his head and tried to get his bearings.

"I said, it would be my pleasure to give you a tour of our city," Oliver said proudly.

"That would be fine, Oliver. Thank you," Maximilian said, although his thoughts were definitely elsewhere.

The two mice emerged into the bright sunlight. Maximilian noticed that the structure that he had landed under was a church.

Maximilian and Oliver walked together down a cobblestone road, alive with early morning activity. Horse-drawn carts bustled down the street as Maximilian worked to dodge feet and wheels alike.

In all honesty, Maximilian was quite frightened. He had never been in a city before. He was beginning to realize why that was. Blades of grass were one thing, but the steel rim of a merchant's wheel was certain to stop a daydream all together.

"You'll notice," Oliver began, seemingly numb to all of the dangers, "that Boston has managed to become the foremost hustling and bustling trading center on the east coast." Oliver was right. Cobblers, tanners, blacksmiths, and artisans of all kinds dotted the city landscape.

"I had no idea that such places even existed," Maximilian responded. "Tanner's Glen is so quiet compared to Boston."

"Well, you get used to it, I suppose," Oliver said.

The two mice proceeded to duck under a set of porch steps and into a small restaurant. It was neatly laid out with several café style tables and chairs. There were already a dozen or so **patrons** when Oliver and Maximilian took a seat. They were immediately approached by a heavy-set mole wearing an apron and an excited expression.

"What do you say, Bigby?" the mole asked, revealing his pleasant disposition.

"How many times do I have to ask you, Vincent? Please call me Oliver," he responded.

"Just can't bring myself to do it, old friend," Vincent said, giving Oliver a friendly pat on the shoulder.

Oliver looked at Maximilian. "Vincent refuses to call me by my first name because I share it with one of England's more **infamous** military generals, Oliver Cromwell."

"Cromwell led the Commonwealth for a time following England's civil war, too."

Vincent was more than happy to add to the conversation.

"What will you gentlemen be having today?" Vincent asked.

"My friend Maximilian and I will both have one of Vincent's finest glasses of water," Oliver said. "Still no tea, I imagine?"

Vincent chuckled as he walked away with his hands on his hips.

"Maximilian," he called back, "that's a nice, strong name."

The commotion of the restaurant was nothing compared to that of the tavern above them. Oliver and Maximilian both arched their necks to take in the conversations.

With so many men talking at the same time, it was impossible to really get any take on what they were discussing. A strategically placed newspaper glared back at them from between the floorboards.

Maximilian strained his eyes and made out the date on the headline.

December 16th . . . 1773.

Chapter 11:
DISBELIEF

Maximilian felt faint. The time machine had transported him not only to the wrong month, but also some 240 years early! It was simply too much for him. The room began to spin and Maximilian blacked out.

He woke to a concerned Oliver kneeling beside him and fanning him with his hat. Oliver helped him back into his chair, where he was able to catch his breath. Maximilian took a sip of his water.

"Are you alright, Maximilian?" Oliver asked in a worried tone. "You look awfully pale."

Maximilian gathered enough energy to reassure Oliver by nodding his head. He had to wait twenty-four hours before the time machine could be restarted again. Even then, Maximilian thought, there was no guarantee that it would work properly. What had he

gotten himself into? What options did he have besides placing his confidence in Nathaniel's time machine for a second time? Maybe it was just a glitch.

Maximilian had made a decision to place his trust in Nathaniel. Now he had to figure out what his next move would be.

Vincent had returned to their table complete with a wet washcloth draped over his arm. "There will be a meeting again tonight at the

South Meeting House," Vincent said quietly to Oliver. "From the sounds of it from my informants upstairs," he said, motioning with his eyes, "something big is in the works."

Oliver nodded. "Maximilian and I will see you there tonight," he said.

Chapter 12:
A BOYCOTT?

Oliver continued his speech as they walked the streets of Boston. But Maximilian's thoughts were elsewhere. The idea that he had been transported to a strange place and time by the time machine was still sinking in as the sun shone brightly through the trees lining the road.

"Over there on the corner is old Jeb Johnson's store," Oliver said, pointing toward a small, modest storefront. The window pane was painted white and Jeb's name was painted in clean, neat font on the glass.

The pair of mice stopped in the shade of a streetlamp. Oliver removed his hat and wiped his brow with his paw.

"Jeb is a perfect example of what most Boston merchants are going through under

King George's reign," Oliver said, turning his attention to Maximilian. "Are you sure you feel alright?" he asked, cocking his head to the side with concern.

"I'm better," Maximilian said. "The fresh air has done wonders." He rolled his shirtsleeves to his elbows and drew a deep breath.

The streets continued to bustle with mid-day traffic. The noise from the carts and horses threatened to drown out Oliver.

"What kind of a store does Mr. Johnson run?" Maximilian inquired.

Oliver motioned for Maximilian to hug the light post closer as several brass-buckled shoes made their way past them.

"Jeb moved here looking to start over for himself and his family," Oliver began. "Sadly, after years of doing quite well for himself, these oppressive Acts are beginning to take their toll on his establishment," he continued in a low voice. "His is a general store, selling many of the things that the British are focusing their taxes on."

In the short time they had spent on the busy side street, no one had gone in or out of Jeb Johnson's General Store. Aside from the small sparrow that sat perched atop the propped open door, the store remained completely quiet.

"So the only hope for Mr. Johnson is that the British laws will be **repealed**?" Maximilian asked. He could certainly understand why so many people were against these unrealistic laws.

How could anyone living in Boston, or the rest of the colonies for that matter, survive? Maximilian began to notice that several other storefronts were empty and closed.

"The Sons of Liberty are doing all that they can," Oliver said with a sigh of frustration. "Parliament passed these regulations to put good people like Jeb out of work. This is what angers us the most."

The brown tree sparrow spread his wings and flew away into the city skyline. As he did, the door to Jeb Johnson's store closed.

Oliver shook his head. "Last week, a **boycott** on all British-made and imported goods was placed throughout the city and the eastern seaboard," Oliver said, placing his hat back firmly on his head.

"What's a boycott?" Maximilian asked as the store went dark and the shades were drawn.

"A boycott is when people and animals are encouraged to stop purchasing certain items — in this case, those made in England," Oliver explained.

That made sense to Maximilian. He guessed that it had to help small local merchants who made their own items.

"Instead, people are encouraged to buy locally made goods or locally grown produce," Oliver continued. "Not only does that help colonial tradesmen like Jeb Johnson, but it also hurts the Crown's finances!"

Both mice seemed pleased with this idea. They hoped that men like Jeb would be able to survive.

"Come," Oliver said, motioning to Maximilian. "There is still one more place I would like to take you before tonight's meeting, and it's getting late."

The afternoon sun was sinking toward the horizon as Oliver and Maximilian continued their journey down the cobblestone road. As they made their way past Jeb Johnson's General Store, the door was locked and a "closed" sign hung in the window.

Chapter 13:
A PATRIOT LIKE PAUL REVERE

Oliver and Maximilian walked in silence down the winding sidewalks. Maximilian's thoughts raced between the time machine, the instructions Nathaniel had given him before he left, and the story Oliver was telling. He realized that Oliver's story eerily resembled his predicament in Tanner's Glen.

Finally they stopped next to a two-story, olive green house with a brick fence in the back. The windows on both floors were decorated with **lattice** and the roof looked to Maximilian as if it had been recently shingled.

"Who lives here?" Maximilian asked.

Oliver placed a paw on Maximilian's shoulder and looked him square in the eyes as he spoke.

"Maximilian," he said, "when desperate times threaten us, certain people and animals take it upon themselves to be part of the solution." The house was dark except for a single candle flickering in the first floor landing.

"When you first arrived in my foundation, you told me the story of Tanner's Glen," Oliver continued. "I could hear the passion in your voice."

Oliver's words struck a chord deep within Maximilian. The mistake by the time machine concerned him, not because of his own safety, but because of the delay it would cause in saving the oak tree and the rest of the forest.

Oliver's paw was firm and reassuring on his back. Maximilian was fortunate to have found a friend in this foreign time and city.

"The man who lives here is a true patriot," Oliver said, motioning toward the house. "His name is Paul Revere. He's one of the leaders of the Sons of Liberty along with the men that you overheard this morning."

The two mice scurried up the side of the brick fence and took their place on the windowsill. Peering inside through the thick glass, Maximilian could see a man sitting alone at a drafting desk. He wiped silt from the window and pressed his nose and whiskers closer.

Revere was a middle-aged man dressed in the same colonial clothing that Maximilian had been seeing since his arrival. He sat with an elbow on his desk and a hand supporting his head, concentrating mightily on a single sheet of paper in front of him.

"What is he working on?" Maximilian asked, not even sure if Oliver knew the answer.

Oliver again turned his attention to Maximilian. "He is preparing for tonight's meeting," he said. "Paul is the light that people like Jeb Johnson look to during these dark times. He is under immense pressure to reassure the people of this fair city and to give them hope for a better tomorrow."

Maximilian continued to watch as Revere traced his quill pen over the parchment. Oliver had taken them far out of their way to show him this spectacle and must have had his reasons.

"And he reminds you of me?" Maximilian asked curiously.

"Yes indeed, young mouse," Oliver said, nodding. "Paul has placed himself in considerable danger being the head of our secret club. The British would love to make an example out of him."

Paul Revere's workshop reminded Maximilian of Nathaniel's. It was littered with tools, oddities, and collectibles. He wondered if Revere wrote by a single flame to avoid bringing attention to his house and his work.

"You are a patriot to your family and to the animals that call Tanner's Glen home," Oliver said, cleaning his glasses. "A mouse who jumped into action when the situation called for it, with little regard for your own safety. You are to be **commended**."

Maximilian paused. He had never thought of what he was doing like that before. He certainly did not consider himself a patriot. He was a simple field mouse doing what anyone would do in the circumstances.

Maximilian watched as Revere closed his eyes. He used his thumb and pointer finger to try to remove the tension and fatigue from his head.

What was he planning? What did he have in mind for Boston and their response to the British? If what Oliver said was true, maybe his solution could shed light on my problems.

"If we are to save ourselves from the greed of the British and the unfair rules they have placed upon us," Oliver said in a serious voice, "Paul Revere will surely play a role in that. Desperate times demand the very best from those willing to lead."

Maximilian knew that these words were intended for him. No one said that saving his home would be easy. He had to be the patriot that Oliver described and defend his home.

The clock at the Old North Church chimed in unison with Maximilian's pocket watch.

"This way, Maximilian," Oliver said with renewed enthusiasm. "It's time for us to join the others."

Chapter 14:
THE SONS OF LIBERTY

A crowd of some two dozen Bostonian animals gathered that evening in the Old South Meeting House. Maximilian, Oliver, and Vincent were among those in the choir balcony. They were waiting patiently to hear from the Sons of Liberty, who had put themselves in great danger by assembling below. The calls of the occasional cricket and harbor loon were the only noises that could be heard over the whispering voices below.

Oliver had taken a break from his usual duty as scribe to give his undivided attention to tonight's agenda. The feeling in the air was that of both tension and anxiety.

Half of Maximilian's attention was in the South Meeting House, while the other half had drifted back to the time machine sitting quietly in Oliver's foundation.

Finally, Samuel stood before the crowd in the church's pulpit. Only a few lanterns were lit for fear that the secret society would be found out by passing British troops or **Loyalists**.

Samuel stood tall before the group.

"Gentlemen," he said, "King George has made it perfectly clear that the interests and the voices of you and our fellow colonists will not be heard during British lawmaking procedure."

Maximilian sat quietly and scanned the crowd. He watched the reactions of both the men and animals attending. Many responded by nodding in agreement.

Oliver leaned over and spoke softly into Maximilian's ear. "This is their fourth meeting this **fortnight**. It is the most I've seen since I've been chronicling the Sons of Liberty."

Samuel used very few hand gestures during his talk. Instead, he stood with his arms sternly crossed over his chest.

"I will give the floor to the distinguished Doctor Aaron James Miller," Samuel said, stepping into the shadows.

A tall, slender man stepped to the front. Maximilian thought he looked painfully thin, maybe even ill, but he addressed the crowd with **conviction**.

"Fellow citizens of Boston, friends of the colonies, I would like to share with you an excerpt from an article that appeared last month in *The London Times* regarding our fair king," Dr. Miller said, adjusting his spectacles.

"Once vigorous measures appear to be the only means left to bringing the Americans to a due submission to the mother country, the colonies will submit," Dr. Miller read. He drew a deep breath and placed his hands on the collar of his overcoat.

"That quote from King George III makes, what we have assumed now for months painfully clear. The taxes placed upon our businesses and the muzzles placed upon our mouths are the only terms that the throne and Parliament are willing to negotiate with anymore."

Dr. Miller took his seat back amongst the crowd. Maximilian looked around and saw the members had begun to discuss this development heatedly.

Maximilian watched as Samuel again appeared. The man hushed the crowd with a single raised hand.

"If our trade be taxed, why not our lands, in short, everything we possess? They tax us without having legal representation," he said. "Tonight, let it be our intention to send a message to all of England. We choose to send this message where they will hear it most—in their purses."

Oliver looked at Maximilian with a large, enthusiastic grin spread across his face.

"Very exciting indeed!" Oliver said.

Maximilian opened his pocket watch. It had been nearly twenty-two hours since he arrived in Boston.

Chapter 15:
BOARDING THE ELEANOR

The evening of December 16, 1773, proved to be a cold one on the banks of the Atlantic Ocean. A large band of patriots, colonists, and animals disguised themselves as Mohawk Indians. They made their way under the cover of night toward Griffin's Wharf.

Maximilian had been given several beaded necklaces, a headdress with a number of brightly dyed feathers, and yellow paint under his eyes. He and the others were armed with wooden-handled axes and hatchets. Bursting from the South Meeting House, they saw the target of the patriots' anger. Three tall British ships belonging to the **East India Company** were anchored in Boston Harbor.

Padded paws and leather moccasins silenced the patriots as they ran. For a while at least, Maximilian's attention was **diverted** from the time machine.

Breathing hard and trying desperately to keep his headdress on, Maximilian shouted to Oliver, "What are we doing exactly?"

The portly brown mouse was only a few steps behind Maximilian, but he was working hard to keep up.

"There are three ships in Boston's harbor, that are the property of Britain's chief trading company," Oliver wheezed.

The moonlight shone brightly through the December clouds. The few residents of Boston who were outside took shelter immediately and bolted their doors. The Sons of Liberty had the overwhelming support of many colonists. But, the fear of British punishment was enough to keep most away from the night's events.

The patriots came to an abrupt stop. Oliver placed his hands on his knees, breathing heavily.

Vincent, who looked as funny as everyone else in his disguise, approached them. He gave Oliver a playful slap on the back.

"How we feeling, Bigby?" he asked.

Oliver responded with a sharp stare.

While Maximilian stood catching his breath, he read the names of the anchored ships aloud, "The *Dartmouth*, the *Eleanor*, and the *Beaver*."

"His Majesty's splendor!" Vincent roared into the cool, crisp night.

Samuel Adams was the first to board. The others quickly followed after him. Once on board, the patriots wasted no time. They began to strike the chests of tea with their axes.

Waiting their turn to board the *Eleanor*, Oliver gave Maximilian some background on the three vessels.

"This royal fleet docked here in November of this year, but it was prevented from unloading its cargo," he began.

"Prevented?" Maximilian asked.

"Indeed," Oliver continued. "Colonists feared that the tea would be seized for failure to pay the **duties**. The tea would end up being

sold on the market, so something had to be done. The colonies first insisted that the tea be returned, but obviously the British were less than willing to comply."

Maximilian scampered up the heavy rope. The excitement of the night was **contagious**. Maximilian was thrilled to be a part of it.

Once he was on the ship, Maximilian glanced back at the shore to see a pawful of spectators looking on in silence. Only the sound of axes splitting wood echoed across the harbor.

"What do we do with the tea once the crates are open?" Maximilian asked Oliver, who was hard at work on a stubborn nail.

"What do we do?" Oliver called back. "Why, we throw it into the sea, of course!"

The scene must have been captivating for those back on the docks. The rebellion would certainly have **repercussions** for weeks to come. The newspaper headlines in both the colonies and on mainland England would have different views on the night's events, but one thing was for sure, there was no turning back now.

Chapter 16:
DUMPING THE TEA

Despite all of the noise, Maximilian could make out the familiar chime of his watch.

Nine o'clock. The time machine would be ready whenever he returned.

By this time, the patriots had emptied some 342 crates of tea into Boston Harbor. They were working quickly to finish their task.

Maximilian could see Vincent as the crowd parted.

"Hey, Maximilian!" Vincent shouted. "Take off your moccasins and empty out all of the tea," he instructed. "Treason is not something one needs to be connected to directly, old chap!"

Word came in short order from the other ships that the decks were to be swept and all evidence of their having been there that night disposed of. The Sons of Liberty made each ship's first mate vow that only the tea cargo was damaged on this historic night.

Maximilian and Oliver made their way down into the first boat departing for shore.

"A glorious night indeed!" Oliver exclaimed.

Maximilian grinned in agreement, although his thoughts were elsewhere.

A gentleman by the name of Lendall Pitts led the patriots, mice included, from the wharf. Maximilian and Oliver walked shoulder-to-shoulder, pleased with how the evening's events had unfolded.

"I'm glad you were here to experience this, Maximilian," Oliver said. "Someday you'll be able to tell your grandmice and great-grandmice that you participated in Boston's—nay the colonies'—biggest night."

A hymn was played as the patriots marched past the home of British Admiral Montague. He had witnessed their work.

Oliver motioned with his tomahawk to an open window overlooking Boston.

"It appears our deeds have not gone unnoticed," he said with a slight chuckle.

Maximilian thought the admiral looked somewhat comical. It was late at night, but he kept his appearance that of midday. He stretched his head out the window, showing his perfect snow-white wig and night coat.

"Well, boys," Montague yelled as they passed by, "you have had a fine, pleasant evening for your Indian caper, haven't you? But mind, you have got to pay the fiddler yet!" His eyes never wavered as he stared sharply on each and every man as they passed.

Chapter 17:
SAYING GOOD-BYE

Oliver and Maximilian bid good night to Vincent, who retired to his home above the café.

"Stop in tomorrow, if you happen to be passing by," Vincent said with a sly wink in Oliver's direction.

"To recount the events of this evening, I assume?" Oliver said proudly.

"Aye, and to have yourself a well-deserved cup of piping hot tea," Vincent chuckled. He opened his oversized paw, revealing two lone mint leaves crumpled into balls.

"Oh no," Oliver said. "You were not supposed to take anything from the boats tonight, Vincent!"

Vincent placed the leaves in his pocket and put his hands on his hips.

"How long have we known one another?" Vincent asked, somewhat offended.

"Long enough." Oliver said suspiciously, "Long enough to be somewhat surprised by this act of thievery."

Vincent took a step toward both mice and spoke to them in a low voice.

"You are absolutely right, my friend," he said. "I'm not like King George. I don't take what's not rightfully mine."

Maximilian looked at Oliver, who appeared both shocked and confused.

"Then, where did you get the mint?" Maximilian asked for both of them.

Vincent drew out a dramatic pause and, unsuccessfully, concealed a growing grin.

"I happened by a friend of mine during tonight's festivities," he explained. "A young meadow vole named Amandine M. Volander. She had trimmed her herb garden today and knew that I had been hard hit by the Tea Act.

This was her way of helping a friend get through a difficult time."

Vincent and Oliver exchanged smiles.

"She's a fine lass this Miss Amandine," Oliver said, pleased to hear that his companion had not taken anything he shouldn't have. "I look forward to that drink, Vincent."

The crowd had nearly gone by this time as the hour was getting very late. The soft leather of their moccasins made no sound as they hurried back to Oliver's home under moonlit skies.

Oliver hummed to himself as they went. He hummed the song that had serenaded them earlier.

Meanwhile Maximilian was getting more and more nervous. The time was fast-approaching when he would put his fate back in Nathaniel's time machine.

Chapter 18:
BACK IN THE TIME MACHINE

O liver opened the door for Maximilian as they returned home to the old foundation. It was very dark and Oliver lit a small lantern.

It was late, but Maximilian was excited to be returning to the time machine. His fur was wet and smelled like a combination of salt water and sweet ocean air.

"Thank you for everything," Maximilian said. He wiped his paw on his vest and extended it to Oliver.

Oliver took it firmly and they embraced.

"Maximilian," Oliver said, "I'm not sure if our paths will ever cross again. But if they do, I look forward to that day very much." He pinched the brim of his three-sided hat and gave it a nod.

Maximilian left Oliver and crawled under the foundation. He climbed into the time machine. Only the tip of Oliver's tail was still visible as Maximilian sat adjusting his seat belt and harness.

So much had happened in the last few hours that Maximilian was finding it difficult to concentrate. He cleared his head and centered his attention again on the numbers that would land him in Tanner's Glen on the correct date this time around.

2013, October, 15, Tanner's Glen.

The hatch closed and Maximilian shut his eyes. Even though he knew what to expect, he was still very nervous.

The time machine began to spin.

Faster . . . faster . . . faster . . . and faster still.

Maximilian's ears began to ring. Finally, the **centrifugal** force eased and Maximilian's lungs yearned for air.

Opening his eyes wide, smoke blocked most of his view. He undid his restraints and stretched his arms. His muscles ached from the stress.

His pocket watch chimed ten.

Maximilian remembered how cold the entire process had made the time machine the first trip. So, he was careful to use his handkerchief to open the latch.

The smoke cleared and Maximilian slowly made his way out of the time machine. His legs buckled as they made contact with the ground. He was very tired. He thought about closing his eyes to sleep, if only for a few minutes.

Maximilian fought the urge to sleep. He looked around in an attempt to take in his new surroundings. He was breathing heavy as his eyes struggled to focus. It appeared that the time machine had come to rest in an attic.

Could he be in the loft of the old Tanner farmhouse?

Beautiful oak beams formed the ceiling that Maximilian gazed up at. A few stray cobwebs decorated the **garret**.

The time machine stood in the corner. Its acorn shell exterior was covered in a layer of frost that was beginning to melt and pool on the floor.

Maximilian noticed a small window and made his way to it. As luck would have it, the fastener turned, the spring released, and it slowly swung open.

The air was cold, like it had been when he left Nathaniel's. He was becoming more and more hopeful that the time machine had worked and he was somewhere on the Tanner homestead.

A nearby storm drain served as the perfect ladder. Maximilian made his way to the dewy grass below.

It was becoming clear to Maximilian that he was in a much more **rural** setting than Boston. A noise on the opposite side of the house caught his attention.

Maximilian moved around the side of the house. He discovered several carriages and wagons making their way past the house. A little drizzle was beginning to fall and storm clouds were gathering in the sky. Maximilian decided to follow the tide of people, being careful to remain out of sight.

He passed by several houses, taverns, and stores, many of which were decorated with red, white, and blue **buntings**. Ahead of him, in the distance, a dark plume of smoke billowed from a black locomotive pulling in to a train depot.

A familiar feeling was beginning to creep into Maximilian's mind—one of despair and hopelessness. The clothing on the people in the streets was different from those of Boston.

But, they were not like the clothes Maximilian was used to seeing around Tanner's Glen.

A large crowd had gathered at the train station by the time Maximilian had arrived. The men, women, and children seemed abuzz. Many were trying desperately to get closer to the loading ramp. Maximilian tried to find a better place by moving behind one of the turnpikes near the railroad tracks.

All at once, the crowd began clapping and cheering. Maximilian strained to see who was getting such a warm welcome. As he did so, a sign above the train depot caught his attention. It was a name, written in bold uppercase lettering . . .

. . .GETTYSBURG.

About the Boston Tea Party

On December 16, 1773, colonist Samuel Adams and a group of Patriots headed for Boston Harbor. Three ships were docked in the harbor, and each carried precious cargo: crates of British tea.

The colonists, known as the Sons of Liberty, were angry because the British government had recently passed the Tea Act. That law made the cost of imported British tea much cheaper than any that was imported by colonial merchants. The colonists rebelled because the government had created a British monopoly on tea, which was unfair to American importers.

Adams and the others demanded that the three ships in Boston Harbor return to England. When they refused, the Sons of Liberty launched what came to be known as the Boston Tea Party. It is considered a crucial act of the American Revolution.

That night, the colonists disguised themselves as Mohawk Indians. They boarded the ships and destroyed 342 crates of tea, dumping the cargo into the ocean. The ships included the *Dartmouth*, the *Eleanor*, and the *Beaver*.

It is said that British Admiral Montague, who had watched the Tea Party from nearby, yelled to the Patriots, "Well, boys, you have had a fine, pleasant evening for your Indian caper, haven't you? But mind, you have got to pay the fiddler yet!"

The British government issued even stricter laws on the colonists soon after. One of those acts closed the port of Boston. Within two years, the Revolutionary War was under way.

Glossary

acquaintance - someone you have met briefly.

alternative - one of the things that can be chosen.

banister - a handrail.

blotter - a book that contains entries waiting to be entered into permanent record.

boycott - to refuse to deal with a person, a store, or an organization until it agrees to certain conditions.

bunting - decoration made of fabric.

canteen - a container for liquid, usually water.

catastrophic - a disastrous end.

centrifugal - an apparent force tending to pull a thing outward when it is rotating around a center.

cherish - to hold dear.

commend - spoken of with approval.

contagious - spreading easily from one person to another.

conviction - the state or appearance of being convinced.

debate - to argue publicly about a question or a topic.

distinguished - celebrated.

divert - to turn aside from a course or direction.

duty - a tax on goods that are being brought into a country.

East India Company - an English company that traded with the East Indies from 1600 to 1874.

eerie - strange or creepy.

emanate - to flow out; to send forth or emit.

engraving - a print made from designs cut into wood, metal, or another material.

famished - to be very hungry.

fortnight - a period of two weeks or fourteen nights.

friction - rubbing of one object or surface against another.

garret - the space, room, or rooms just below the roof of a house.

hearth - the floor of a fireplace.

imperative - absolutely necessary.

infamous - having or causing a bad name or image for oneself; shameful.

inherit - to receive from a person.

injustice - the violation of the rights of another person.

intricately - full of detail or puzzling parts.

lattice - a structure of crossed wood or metal strips.

levy - to impose.

Loyalist - a colonist who was loyal to the British government during the American Revolution.

meticulous - extremely careful about details.

offset - something that shows off another item.

Parliament - the national legislative body of Great Britain, composed of the House of Commons and the House of Lords.

patron - one who supports an individual or a cause with money, resources, or influence.

precariously - dependent on chance.

predicament - a difficult situation.

regiment - a military unit consisting of two or more battalions and forming a basic element of a division.

repeal - to formally withdraw or cancel.

repercussion - a far-reaching, often indirect effect of or reaction to some event or action.

rural - relating to the country or farmland.

scribe - a writer.

silhouette - the outline of a figure or profile.

Stamp Act - first British tax in 1765 on goods and services, including wills, newspapers, and playing cards.

Sugar Act - a British act in 1764 that halved the duty on foreign-made molasses, placed duties on certain imports that had not been taxed before, and strengthened the enforcement of the law.

talons - the claws of a bird of prey.

tariff - a tax placed on imported goods.

Tea Acts - British acts in 1773 that gave the East India Company special rights in the colonial tea business.

Townshend Acts - British acts in 1767 that taxed certain colonial imports and stationed troops at major colonial ports to protect customs officers.

transfix - to make motionless.

transcend - to go beyond the limits of something.

waistcoat - a vest.

About the Author

Maximilian P. Mouse, Time Traveler was created by Philip M. Horender. Horender resides in upstate New York with his wife, Erin, and their dog, MoJo.

Horender earned his Bachelor of Arts in History with a minor in education from St. Lawrence University. He later obtained his Masters in Science in Education from the University at Albany, the State University of New York.

He currently teaches high school history, coaches swimming, and advises his school's history club. When he is not writing, Horender enjoys biking, kayaking, and hiking with Erin and MoJo.